To Meredith Mundy, editor extraordinaire,
for her wonderful insight, creativity, and kindness.
Thanks for believing in me! —K.K.O.

For my nephew Keon, who brings so much joy to our family.
And with gratitude to my fiancé and family
for their unwavering love.—Z.C.

STERLING CHILDREN'S BOOKS
New York

An Imprint of Sterling Publishing Co., Inc.
1166 Avenue of the Americas
New York, NY 10036

Text © 2019 Karen Kaufman Orloff
Illustrations © 2019 Ziyue Chen

ISBN 978-1-4549-2620-7

Distributed in Canada by Sterling Publishing Co., Inc.
c/o Canadian Manda Group, 664 Annette Street
Toronto, Ontario M6S 2C8, Canada
Distributed in the United Kingdom by GMC Distribution Services
Castle Place, 166 High Street, Lewes, East Sussex BN7 1XU, England
Distributed in Australia by NewSouth Books
University of New South Wales, Sydney, NSW 2052, Australia

For information about custom editions, special sales, and premium and corporate purchases,
please contact Sterling Special Sales at 800-805-5489 or specialsales@sterlingpublishing.com.

Manufactured in China

Lot #:
2 4 6 8 10 9 7 5 3 1
11/18

sterlingpublishing.com

The artwork for this book was created digitally.
Design by Ryan Thomann

# SOME DAYS

by
## KAREN KAUFMAN ORLOFF
illustrated by
## ZIYUE CHEN

STERLING CHILDREN'S BOOKS
New York

Some days
are chocolate pudding pie days.

Kites up in the sky days.

Jumping super high days.

Some days are swim at Grandpa Joe's days.

Water through my toes days.

Take a little doze days.

Some days are
hurt myself somehow days.

Icky . . . sticky . . . **OW!** . . . days.

Need my mommy *now* days.

Some days are picking out a pup days.

Win a shiny cup days.

Getting all dressed up days.

Some days are Mommy makes a fuss days.

Running for the bus days.

No kickball for us days.

Some days are angels in the snow days.

Rolling out the dough days.

Watch a fire glow days.

Some days are waiting at the store days.

Make a mess of
chore days.

Daddy yells,
"No more!"
days.

Some days are feeling kind of mad days.

Sorry to be
bad days.

Just a little
sad days.

Some days are
digging in the dirt days.

Point a hose
and squirt days.

Going for dessert days.

Some days are getting rid of fleas days.

Drippy nose
and sneeze days.

Running from the bees days.

Some days are
playing on my own days.

Kicking up a stone days.

Feeling all alone days.

But MOST days are . . .

Ready? One, two, three days!

Lots to do and see days.

Learning to be me days.